LITTLE TREE

e.e. cummings

LITTLE TREE

illustrated by Deborah Kogan Ray

Crown Publishers, Inc., New York

To Barbara and Clarke
many Christmases
many little trees

Text copyright 1923, 1925, renewed 1951, 1953 by E.E. Cummings. Copyright
©1973, 1976 by the Trustees for the E.E. Cummings Trust. Copyright ©1973, 1976
by George James Firmage.
Illustrations copyright ©1987 by Deborah Kogan

Published by Crown Publishers, Inc., 225 Park Avenue South, New York, New York
10003 and represented in Canada by the Canadian MANDA Group.
CROWN is a trademark of Crown Publishers, Inc.
Manufactured in Japan

Library of Congress Cataloging-in-Publication Data
Cummings, E. E. (Edward Estlin), 1894-1962. Little tree. Summary: The poet/
individualist's ode to a small tree decorated for Christmas and proud to receive
admiring attention. 1. Christmas trees—Juvenile poetry. 2. Children's poetry,
America. [1. Christmas trees—Poetry. 2 American poetry] I. Ray, Deborah, ill.
II. Title.
PS3505.U334L5 1987   811'.52   86-30940
ISBN 0-517-56598-6

10 9 8 7 6 5 4 3 2 1

First Edition

little tree
little silent Christmas tree
you are so little
you are more like a flower

who found you in the green forest
and were you very sorry to come away?

see   i will comfort you
because you smell so sweetly

i will kiss your cool bark
and hug you safe and tight
just as your mother would,
only don't be afraid

look   the spangles
that sleep all the year in a dark box
dreaming of being taken out and allowed to shine,

the balls the chains red and gold the fluffy threads,

put up your little arms
and i'll give them all to you to hold
every finger shall have its ring
and there won't be a single place dark or unhappy

then when you're quite dressed
you'll stand in the window for everyone to see
and how they'll stare!
oh but you'll be very proud

and my little sister and i will take hands
and looking up at our beautiful tree
we'll dance and sing
"Noel Noel"

little tree
little silent Christmas tree
you are so little
you are more like a flower

who found you in the green forest
and were you very sorry to come away?
see   i will comfort you
because you smell so sweetly

i will kiss your cool bark
and hug you safe and tight
just as your mother would,
only don't be afraid

look   the spangles
that sleep all the year in a dark box
dreaming of being taken out and allowed to shine,
the balls the chains red and gold the fluffy threads,

put up your little arms
and i'll give them all to you to hold
every finger shall have its ring
and there won't be a single place dark or unhappy

then when you're quite dressed
you'll stand in the window for everyone to see
and how they'll stare!
oh but you'll be very proud

and my little sister and i will take hands
and looking up at our beautiful tree
we'll dance and sing
"Noel Noel"